It's Checkup and Vaccination Time!

BY DR. KETTLEN BORDA, MD

Illustrated by Carla Saavedra B.

Disclaimer:

This book is for general educational purposes only. It does not provide any medical advice for any adult or children. Information and recommendations regarding your health and vaccinations should be given to you by a qualified healthcare provider who knows you. It is also not intended to guide medical practice. The author does not assume any responsibility for how the information in this book is used.

It's Checkup and Vaccination Time!
Published 2021.
ISBN: 978-65-00-33913-0

Reference: Growth Chart developed by the Department of Health and Human Services, Centers for Disease Control and Prevention, National Center for Health Statistics. http://www.cdc.gov/growthcharts. Retrieved from https://wicworks.fns.usda.gov/resources/wic-growth-charts on October 19, 2021.

To my sons and to every pediatric patient.

Tony was having fun at the park. While he was playing, his mom received a call from Dr. Lara's office reminding her of Tony's appointment the next day.

When he finished swirling down the slide, he heard his mom saying,

"All right, I will bring his **vaccination card.**"

When she finished the call, Tony asked,

"Mommy, what is a **vaccination card**?"

"That's a good question, Tony," she said. "A vaccination card is where we keep track of all the vaccines we receive."

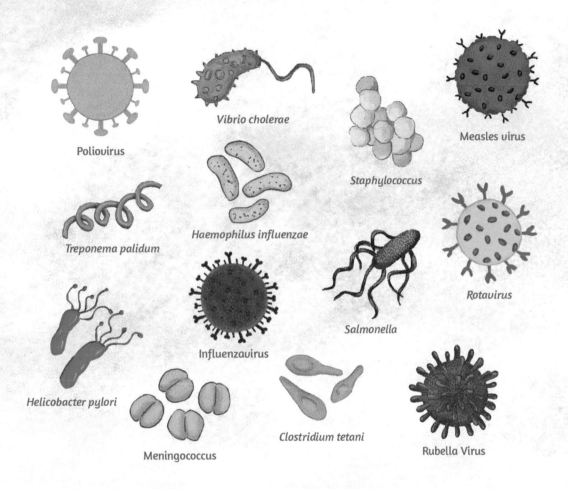

Poliovirus

Vibrio cholerae

Staphylococcus

Measles virus

Haemophilus influenzae

Treponema palidum

Rotavirus

Influenzavirus

Salmonella

Helicobacter pylori

Meningococcus

Clostridium tetani

Rubella Virus

"But Mommy, what is a **vaccine**?"
Tony asked.

"A vaccine is a type of medicine that helps our bodies fight super tiny bugs that can make us very sick," she explained.

"Okay, Mommy," said Tony. "So, who called you asking about the vaccination card?"

"The doctor's office called to remind me to bring your vaccination card since you are going to be vaccinated tomorrow," his mom replied.

"That's good," said Tony. "Are they going to give me a pill?"

His mom answered, "Tony, I wish vaccines were pills, but most vaccines are given by an **injection shot**—like a tiny poke in your skin."

"Oh, really, Mommy?" Tony asked. "So, is it going to hurt?"

"Probably, Tony," she said. "But it should be super quick, and you shouldn't worry because I'm going to be there with you. You're going to be all right."

The next day was Tony's appointment. On the way to the clinic, his mom said, "Tony, remember that Mommy is going to be there with you. The vaccination will be very quick, and I will give you a big hug as soon as we are done."

They arrived at the **pediatric clinic**. Tony loved looking at the little animals and trees painted on the walls of the waiting area while his mom filled out some papers.

Not too long after they arrived, Nurse Olivia said, "Hello, Tony. Welcome back! Come over this way. We're going to check a couple of things before we go into the **examination room**."

First, Nurse Olivia checked Tony's **height**.

Then, she checked his **weight**.

Lastly, she checked his **vision**.

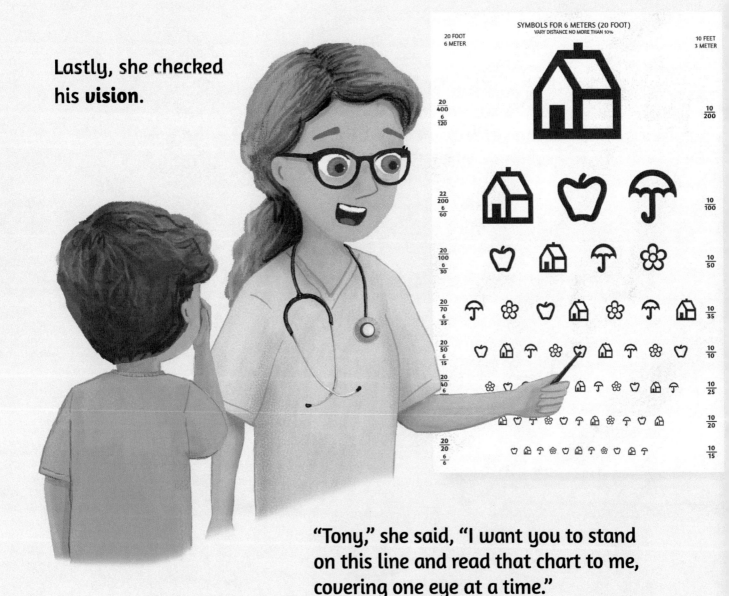

SYMBOLS FOR 6 METERS (20 FOOT)
VARY DISTANCE NO MORE THAN 10%

20 FOOT
6 METER

10 FEET
3 METER

20/400 6/120 — 10/200

22/200 6/60 — 10/100

20/100 6/30 — 10/50

20/70 6/35 — 10/35

20/50 6/15 — 10/10

20/40 6 — 10/25

— 10/20

20/20 6/6 — 10/15

"Tony," she said, "I want you to stand on this line and read that chart to me, covering one eye at a time."

Tony read through the chart and Nurse Olivia said, "Thank you, Tony!"

They then went to Dr. Lara's office and Nurse Olivia said, "While we wait for Dr. Lara, I'm going to check your **blood pressure**. I will wrap this cuff around your arm, and you will feel a squeeze. It won't take long."

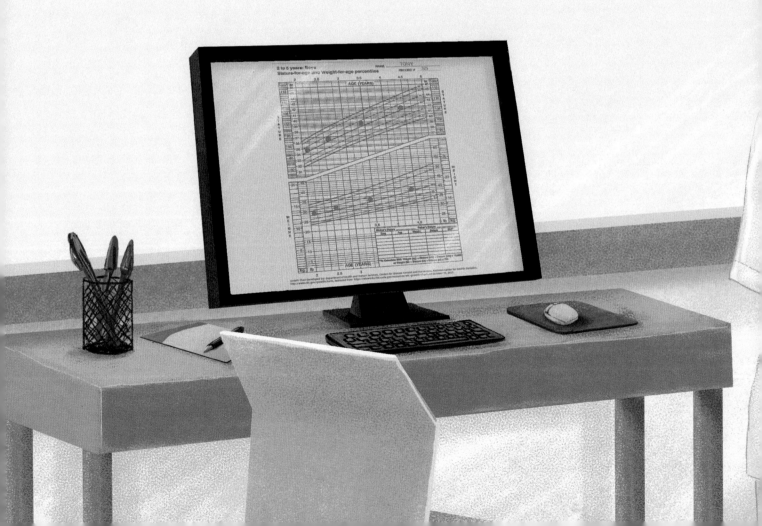

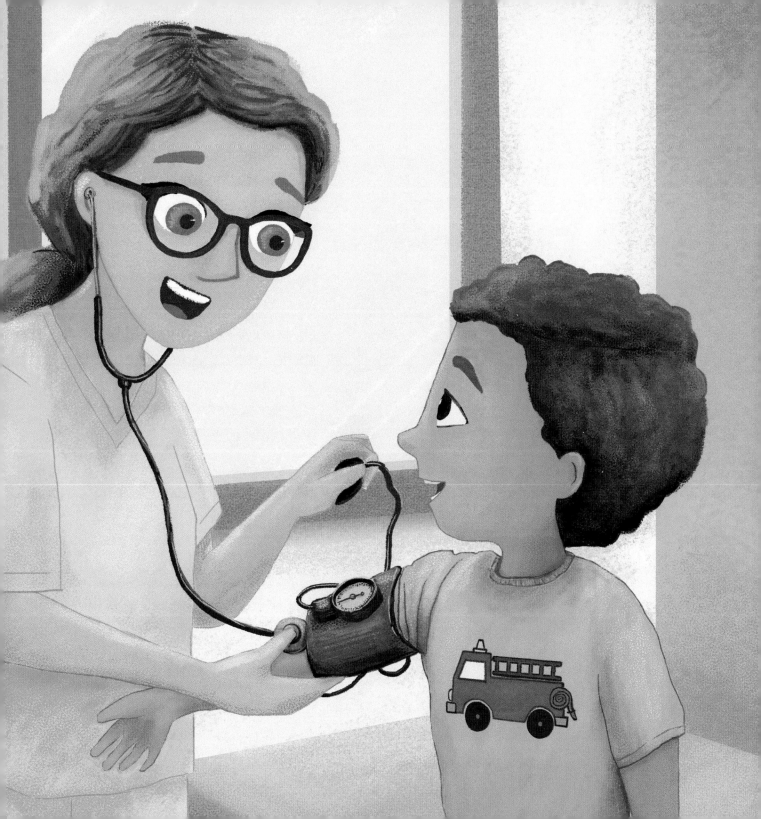

Dr. Lara came into the room with a big smile and said,

"Hi, Tony! It is so good to see you again! You've grown a lot since I saw you last year. How are you doing?"

"Hi, Dr. Lara! I'm doing well, thank you!" Tony replied.

Dr. Lara asked Tony and his mom some questions and then told Tony,

"Come over to the table so I can examine you."

Tony said, "Okay, Dr. Lara."

She started by listening to his **heart** with her stethoscope.

Then, she listened to his **lungs**. "Take deep breaths, in and out . . . Everything sounds great, Tony!" she said.

She also checked Tony's **tummy**.

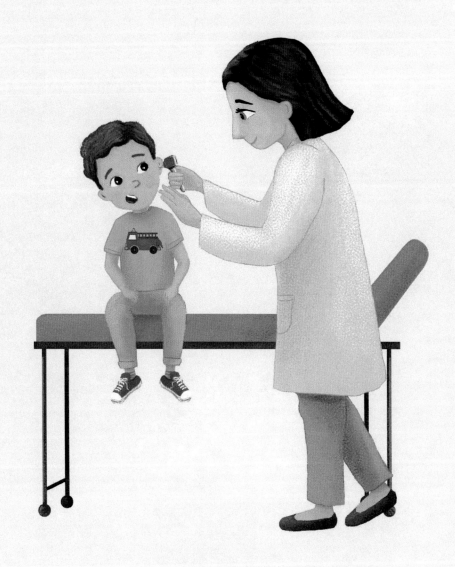

Then, she looked inside his **ears**
with her otoscope

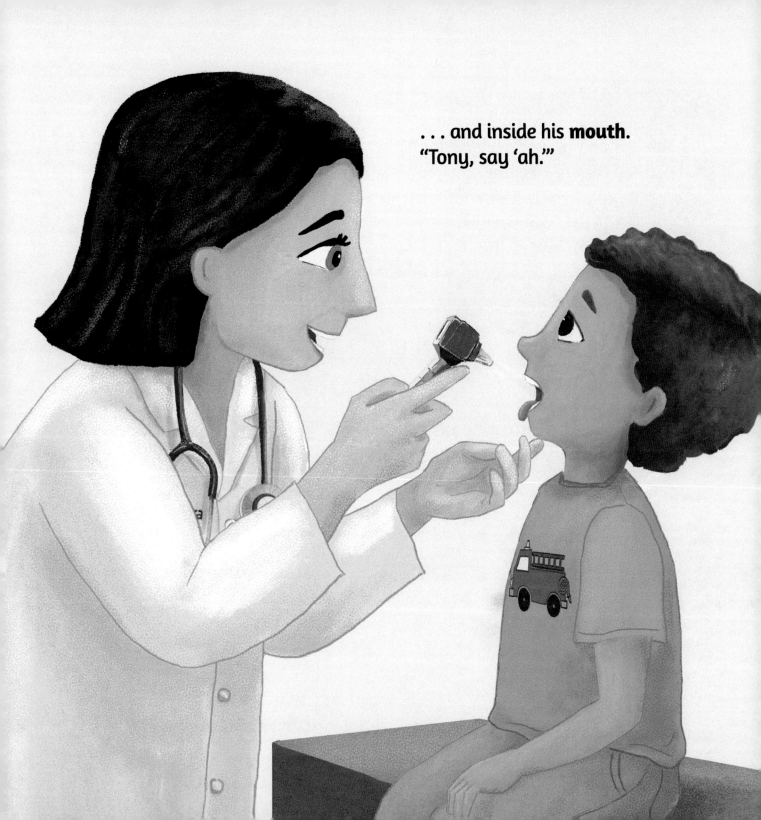

. . . and inside his **mouth**.
"Tony, say 'ah.'"

At the end of the exam, Dr. Lara said,

"Tony, thank you for coming today. I can see that you're taking good care of your health. Keep eating your **fruits** and **vegetables**, **sleeping** well, and **playing** a lot so you can continue to grow healthy! When I leave, Nurse Olivia will give you your vaccines, and you'll be ready to go. I'll see you again in a year."

"Thank you, Dr. Lara. See you in a year!" Tony said.

Nurse Olivia then said,

"Tony, I have the **vaccines** ready, and I also have these pretty bandages to put on when I am done."

"Oh, I like them!" he said, looking at the colorful **bandages**.

"It will be very quick, I promise you," she said.

"Okay," Tony replied.

Nurse Olivia counted:

"One, two, three . . . Done!"

"Now, let's just put the bandages on."

"Mommy, it wasn't too bad, but I still want my hug," Tony said.

"Of course, Tony," his mom said. "Let me give you a big hug. You are so brave!"

PEDIATRICS

Before they left the clinic, Nurse Olivia handed them some papers with the summary of that visit and Tony's vaccination card. After that, they were all done—and Tony was thankful that they were all helping him to be healthy and happy.

About the Author

Kettlen Borda is a physician, but she also holds bachelor's degrees in Biological Sciences and Nutrition Science. She is married to Guilherme Borda, and they have two young sons. She enjoys spending time with her family in nature, cooking healthy foods, going to church, and visiting friends.

Please, visit her website at www.kettlen.com for updates.

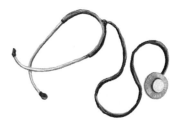

Made in the USA
Middletown, DE
21 December 2021

56790676R00024